Miss Sadie McGee who Lived in a Tree

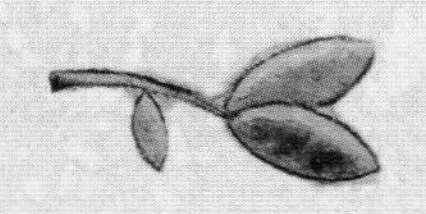

ISBN-13: 978-0-8249-5152-8
ISBN-10: 0-8249-5152-2

Published by Ideals Children's Books
An imprint of Ideals Publications
535 Metroplex Drive, Suite 250
Nashville, Tennessee 37211
www.idealsbooks.com

Color separations by Precision Color Graphics, Franklin, Wisconsin

Printed and bound in China

Library of Congress Cataloging-in-Publication Data

Moulton, Mark Kimball.
Miss Sadie McGee who lived in a tree / written by Mark Kimball Moulton ; illustrated by Karen Hillard Good.
p. cm.
Summary: Many people wonder why Sadie McGee lives in a tree overlooking the sea, but only one person knows the truth.
ISBN 0-8249-5152-2 (alk. paper)
[1. Eccentrics and eccentricities—Fiction. 2. Trees—Fiction. 3. Coasts—Fiction. 4. Stories in rhyme.] I. Good, Karen Hillard, ill. II. Title.
PZ8.3.M8622Mis 2005
[E]—dc22
2005026059

10 9 8 7 6 5 4 3 2

Designed by Eve DeGrie, Karen Hillard Good, and Georgina Chidlow-Rucker

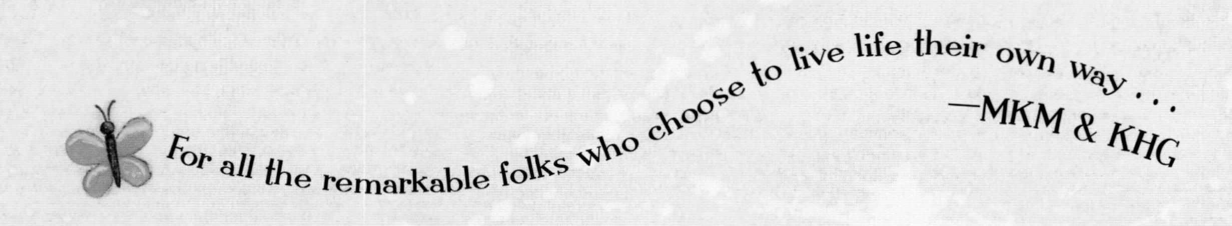

Miss Sadie McGee who Lived in a Tree

Written By Mark Kimball Moulton

Illustrated By Karen Hillard Good

ideals children's books.
Nashville, Tennessee

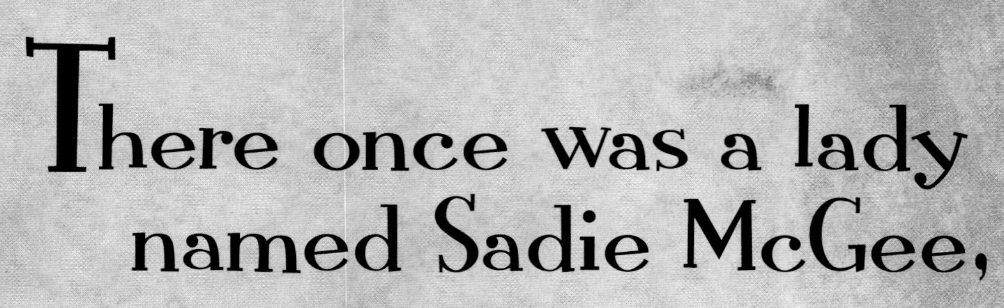

There once was a lady named Sadie McGee,

a kindly old woman of great mystery,
who lived in the top of a hickory tree
on a cliff overlooking the sea.

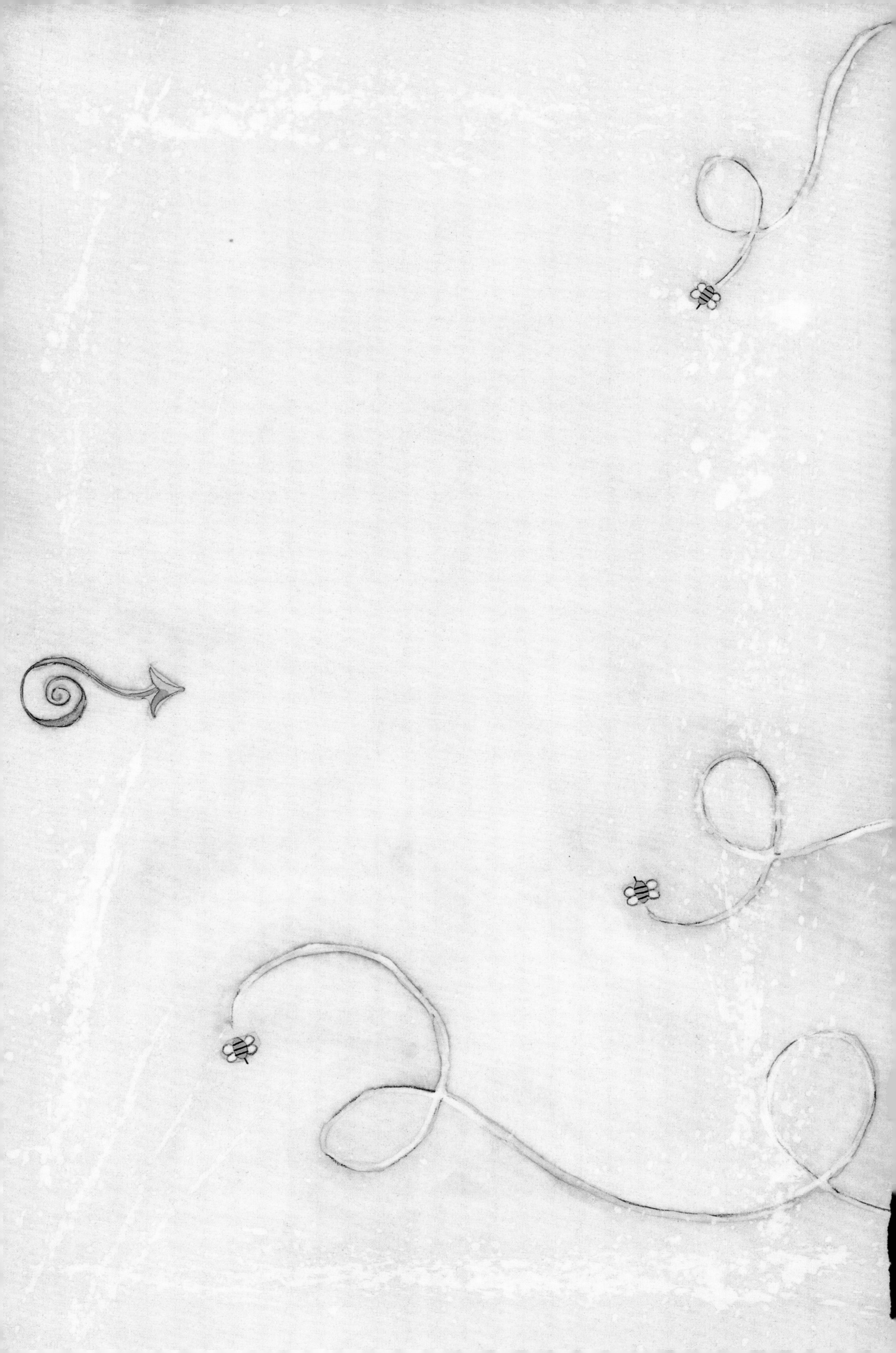

Folks from all over the world came to see
this remarkable lady, this Sadie McGee,
for no one had seen such a rare oddity
as a lady who lived in a tree.

They'd stand underneath, somewhat curiously,
bending this way and that way, the better to see
this peculiar old lady of great mystery,
who lived in a tree by the sea.

There it is! Sadie's tree!
Oi, Vai!
Kosher Dill
KOSHER DELI
arf!
?
Hey, girl... How'd You git up there?

They'd peer through the
branches at Sadie McGee,
as she cooked and she cleaned
in her tree, happily,

And they'd ask one
another, inquisitively,
"Why does she live
up in a tree?"

But no one could answer,
none under the tree
could explain how or why
this Miss Sadie McGee
came to live all alone
in that hickory tree,
on that cliff
overlooking the sea.
Nobody, that is,
except me!

why?
Why does she live in a tree?
For once, long ago, I met Miss McGee, on a bright, sunny day that was slightly windy, as I picnicked beneath that magnificent tree, overlooking the sparkling sea.
Can you see anything?

I was running along
on that cliff by the sea,
with my bright yellow kite
flying high behind me,
when a big gust of wind
came along suddenly,
and my kite ended up
in that tree.

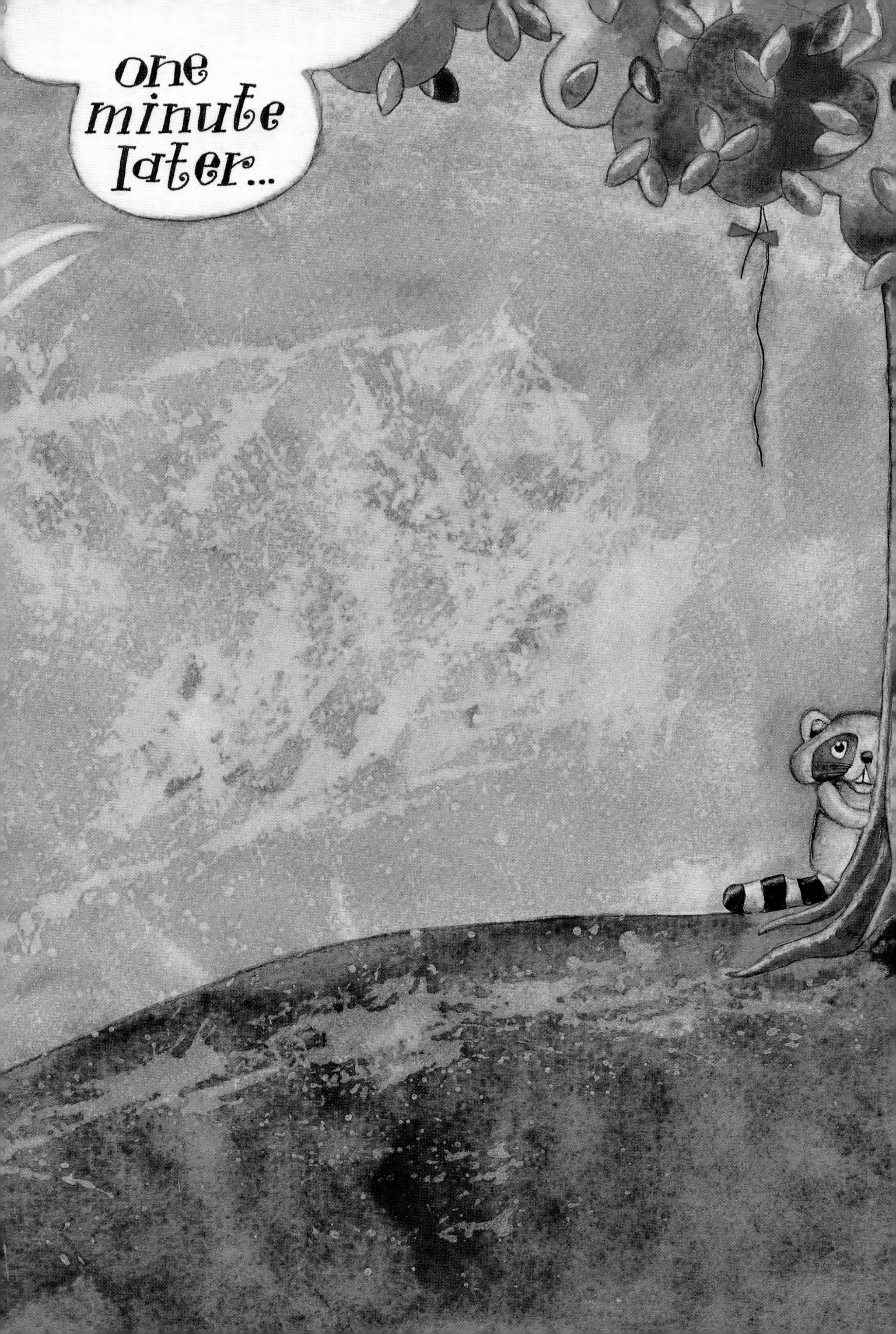
one minute later...

I stood underneath
and peered up, quizzically,
bending this way and that way,
the better to see
my poor kite that was lodged
at the top of the tree,
and I wondered how this
came to be—

My day ruined by this kite-stealing tree!

The frustration I felt
got the better of me.
I'm ashamed to admit
that I acted silly,

and kicked at the trunk
of the kite-stealing tree,
and I cried,
"Give my
kite
back
to me!"

"I'm very sorry," said the tree, cordially.
"I will happily help you to set your kite free.
Won't you come up and join me for hickory tea?
Use the door. I will throw down the key."

And with that, from the leaves
at the top of the tree,
a plump, rosy face poked
straight through, suddenly,
(so it wasn't the tree that
was talking to me)
and that's when I first met Sadie—
the kindly old Sadie McGee.

She tossed me a key that was slightly rusty,
which I tried in the lock in the door in the tree,
and the door in the tree opened up, squeakily,
and I entered the tree warily.

The stairs in the tree of Miss Sadie McGee
twisted this way and that way and made me dizzy,
but I came to the top eventually,
and I thanked Miss McGee breathlessly.

Thanks!
Almost there!

GO
SLOW

HONEY
She's really nice.

As promised, she'd put
on the kettle for tea,
which she served graciously
to three squirrels and to me,
and we sat on a branch
most companionably,
and she told me
how she came to be

"The Old Lady Who Lives in a Tree."

It seems there was once a young Mistah McGee
who had promised he'd lasso the moon for Sadie,
but instead, Miss McGee (who was then Miss McVie)
asked to live in a tree by the sea—

the moon wouldn't make her happy.

"In fact," she continued, unabashedly,
"I'm surprised that you missed my old Mistah McGee,
on your way up the stairs for your visit with me,
since he lives in the base of this tree."

But that is
another story.
I hoped one day
she'd tell it to me.

The time slipped away as time does by the sea,
and the clock in the tree chimed a quarter to three.
We raised our eyebrows, just as surprised as could be
that the time had flown by so quickly.

I bowed low and I thanked my new friend, Miss McGee,
for retrieving my kite from the top of her tree,
and of course for the tea and the view of the sea,
which in all honesty was most heavenly,

and I left.

So the answer to why kindly Sadie McGee
lived her life all alone way up high in a tree,
on a cliff overlooking the glittering sea,
is quite simple, a near certainty.

At least it is simple to me.

For this lady, Miss Sadie, loved life in her tree,
with the fluffy gray squirrels
who would stop by for tea,
and the beautiful birds that sang beautifully,
and the occasional bumbling bee.

You see—

Home Sweet Home

That old hickory tree
was just right for Sadie.
It was all that she wanted
and where she should be.
Close your eyes and imagine.
I think you'll agree
that Miss Sadie McGee was lucky.

In the mornings she'd wake
and she'd gaze out to sea,
watch the dolphins and whales
swimming by gracefully,
wave to sailors on ships
who waved back merrily,
as they went on another journey.

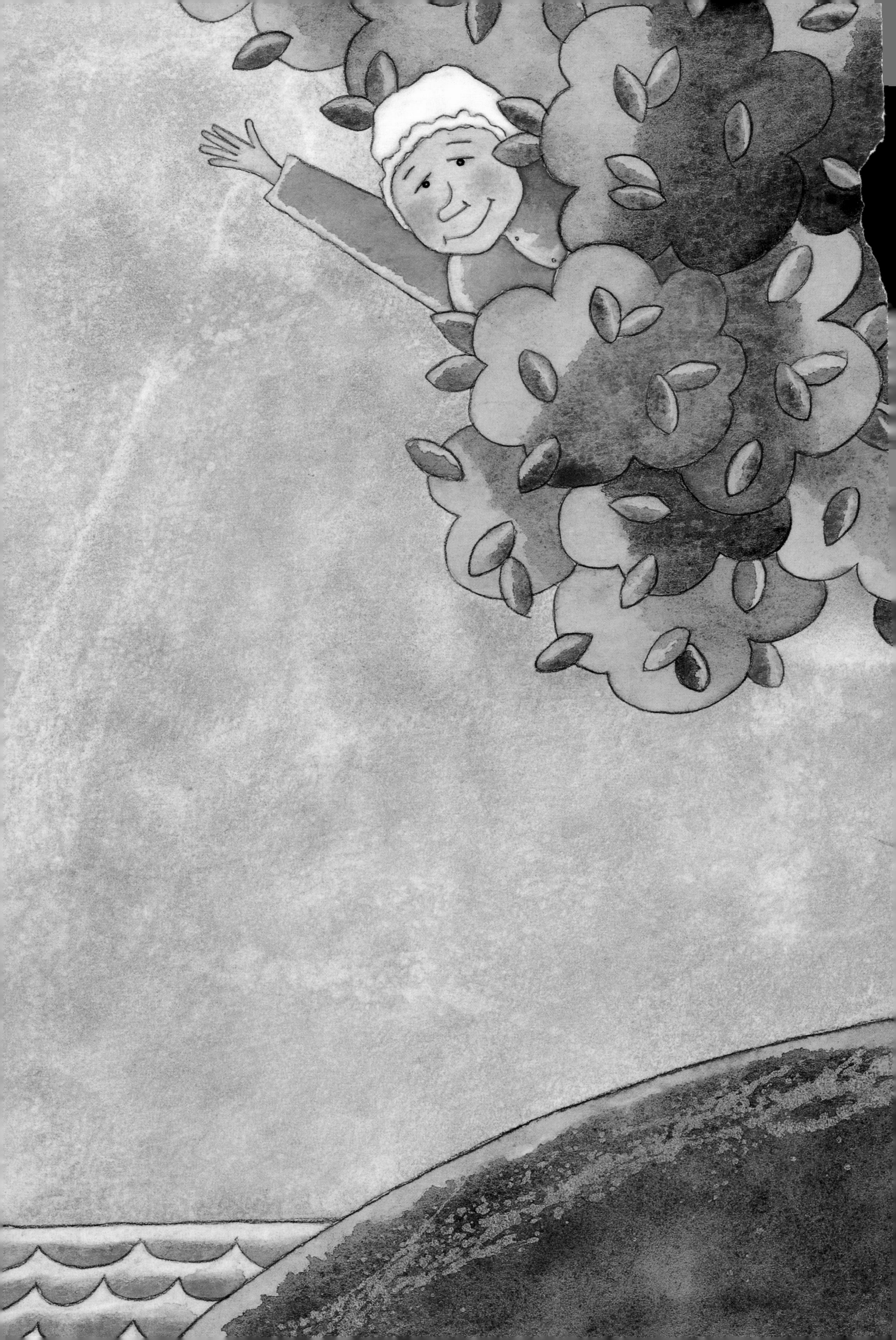

And at night Miss McGee
rocked to sleep blissfully,
in her bed on a branch
of that hickory tree,
while the breeze through the leaves
softly sang to Sadie,
and the stars twinkled on peacefully.

So she wasn't alone, not Miss Sadie McGee!
Why, in fact, I would venture, most confidently,
that Miss Sadie McGee lived contentedly,
in that hickory tree by the sea.

For she chose to live life her own way, modestly,
peacefully, comfortably, and generously,
with her squirrels and her birds and occasional bee,
way up high in her great, big, old tree,
overlooking the shimmering sea.

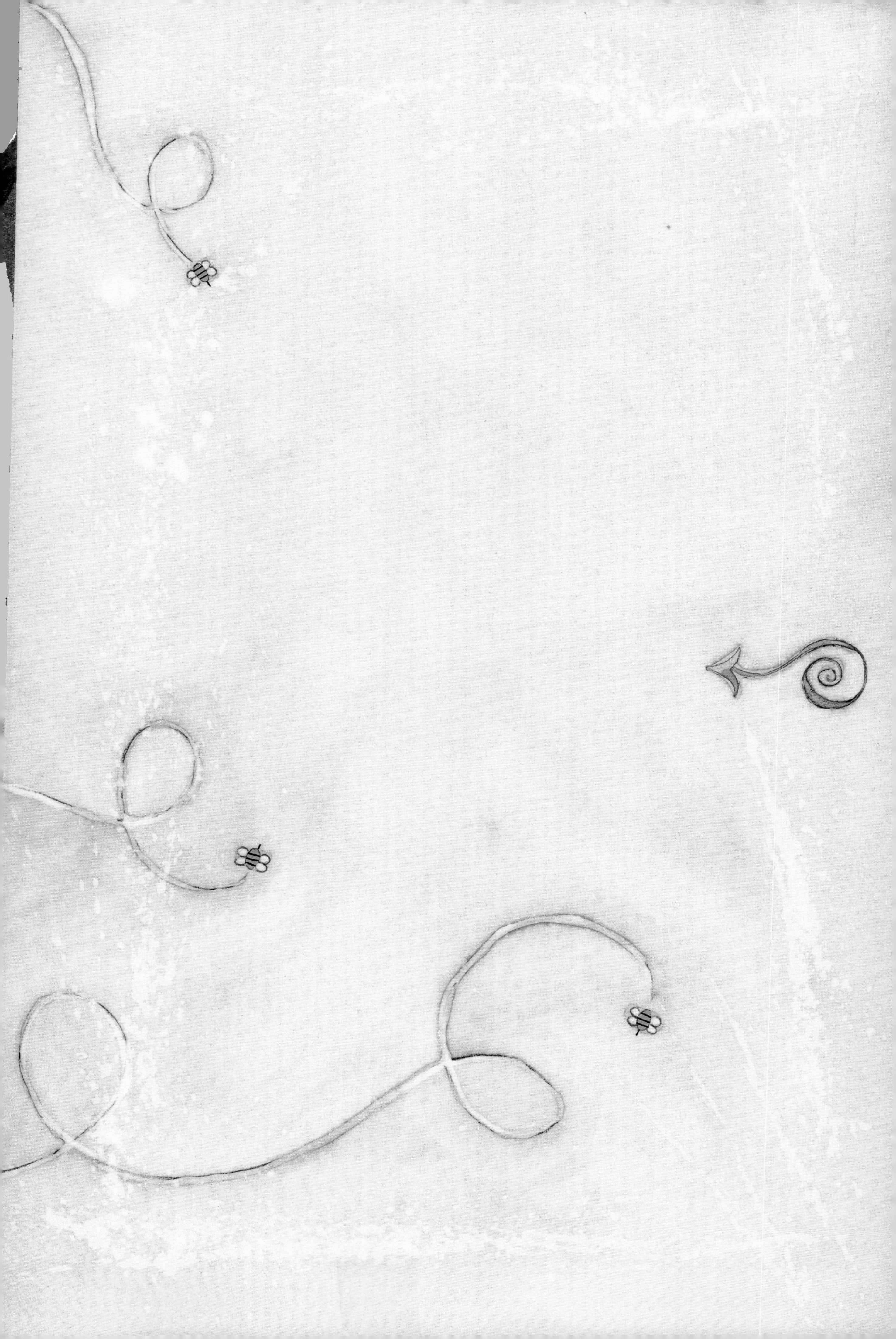

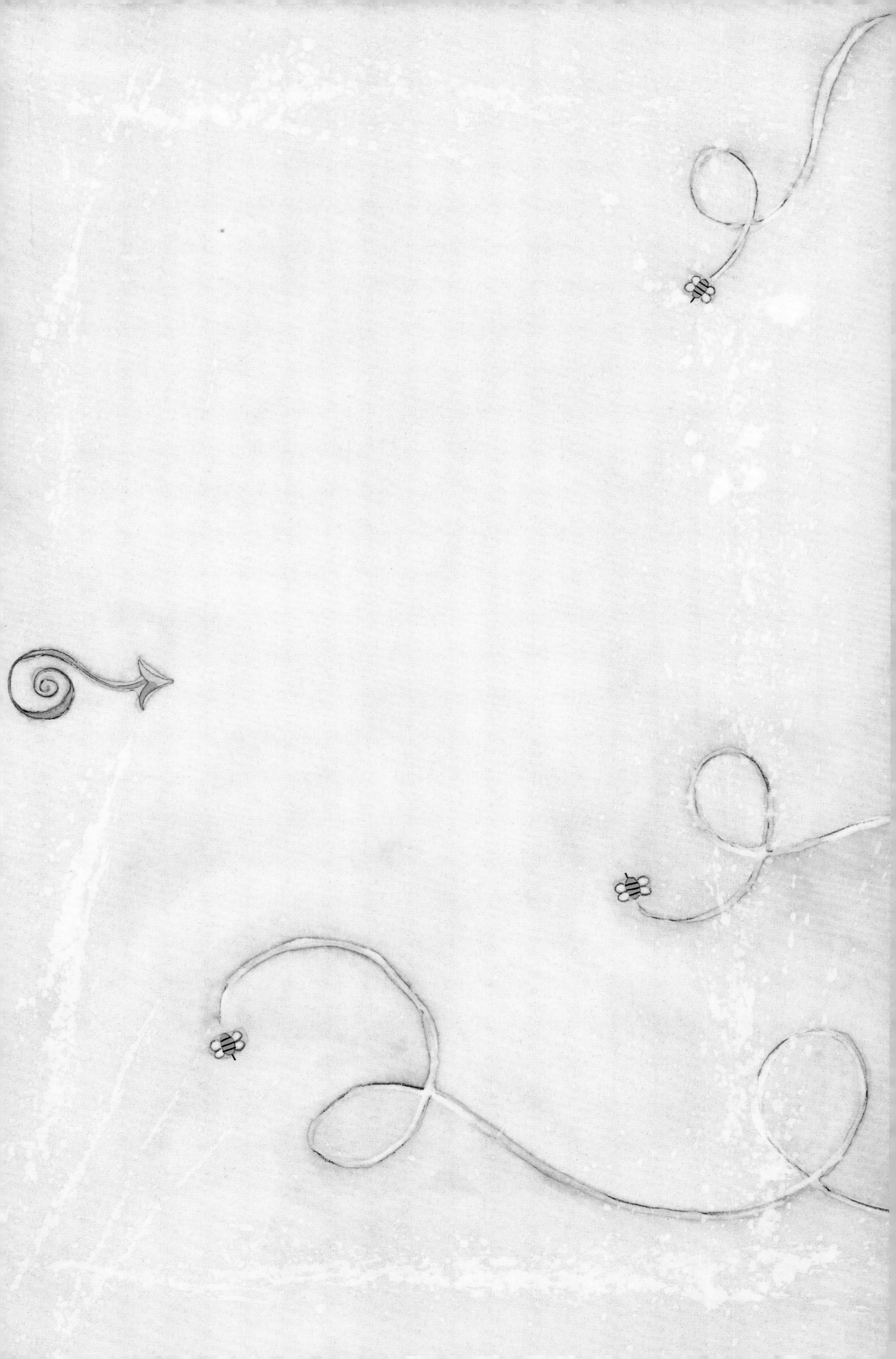

And that was enough
for Miss Sadie McGee.